D0300060

Co
Libra

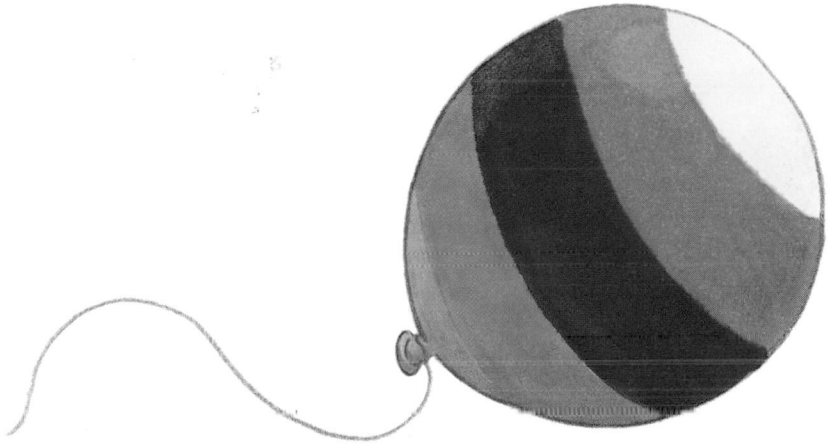

BALLOON

Sch

NORTHAMPTONSHIRE LIBRARIES
BFS 07 DEC 2001
F

For Judy and Larry

First published in hardback in Great Britain by HarperCollins Publishers Ltd in 1998.
First published in Picture Lions in 1999.

7 9 10 8 6
ISBN 0 00 664 624-7

Picture Lions is an imprint of the Children's Division, part of HarperCollins Publishers Ltd,
77-85 Fulham Palace Road, Hammersmith, London W6 8JB.

Text and illustrations copyright © Jez Alborough 1998.
The author asserts the moral right to be identified as the author of the work.
A CIP catalogue record for this title is available from the British Library.
All rights reserved. No part of this publication may be reproduced,
stored in a retrieval system or transmitted in any form or by any means,
electronic, mechanical, photocopying, recording or otherwise,
without the prior permission of HarperCollins Publishers Ltd,
77-85 Fulham Palace Road, Hammersmith, London, W6 8JB.

Printed and bound in Singapore by Imago.

BALLOON

Jez Alborough

Collins

An imprint of HarperCollins*Publishers*

Billy saw it

Mummy bought it

Man threw it

Billy caught it.

Billy pulled it and waved it

Billy headed

and saved it.

Billy squeezed it

Billy tossed it

Billy missed it and lost it.

Mummy saw it

Mummy chased it

Dog barked

Dog raced it.

Dog jumped

Dog whacked it

Duck quacked...

and attacked it.

Cow licked it

Cow flicked it

Cow mooed and Cow kicked it. Bird flipped it

and flapped it Tree tangled and trapped it.

Wind threw it

Wind caught it

Wind blew it

and...

...brought it.

Billy chased it

Billy...

...stopped it.

But tripped up

and...

BA

NG

popped it.

Mummy sighed, Dog looked glum, Billy saw...

another one!